Healing for the Heart…
A Guide for Survival
In the World of the
Widow

By
Nancy E. Hughes

Copyright © 2007 by Nancy E. Hughes

Healing for the Heart... A Guide for Survival in the World of the Widow
by Nancy E. Hughes

Printed in the United States of America

ISBN 978-1-60266-974-1

All rights reserved solely by the author. The author guarantees all contents are original and do not infringe upon the legal rights of any other person or work. No part of this book may be reproduced in any form without the permission of the author. The views expressed in this book are not necessarily those of the publisher.

Unless otherwise indicated, Bible quotations are taken from Ryrie Study Bible Expanded Edition. Copyright © 1984 by International Bible Society.

www.xulonpress.com

Dedication

This book is dedicated to
LeRoy
my love, my friend, my prayer partner
and to
Tyler , Leigh and Lindsay
for encouraging me to Praise the Lord
on paper

Outline

Nancy describes the world known as "Widowhood" and how she became a member of this exclusive club. She shares suggestions for members as well as non-members of the club.

Jacque was thrown violently into the membership in the widow club. She shares how to deal with children and the death of a parent. She also offers encouragement to those struggling through the days and weeks after the death of a husband.

Saundra was suddenly dumped into the world of the widow. She addresses the loneliness that follows a widow and how to handle comments from people who are not members of the club.

Betty shares how to cope with the loss of a husband after 63 years of marriage to her best friend. She describes ways of coping in the weeks and months after joining the club.

Kay only had 8 weeks to deal with the reality of losing her husband. She discusses the reality that we live in a "couples" world that does not include widows.

Linda gives advice to those who want to know how to help in the healing process that must take place when losing one's husband.

Jo was the mother of two small girls when she took her first breath as a widow. She shares lessons on dealing with grief when others depend on you for everything they need.

Introduction

On a hot August afternoon, with no warning, I was instantly and unceremoniously initiated into the club known as "Widowhood." No one asked me if I wanted to join. No one asked my permission to place my membership with this club. No one explained what would happen once I became a member. The clubhouse door was opened and I was thrown into a world unlike any other I had ever experienced. No explanation. No instructions. No encouragement.

I joined the widow ranks early and unexpectedly. Before that time I had felt a great deal of sympathy toward women who had lost their spouses. I just never truly understood how my life would totally change and absolutely could NOT have predicted how other people would respond to me...without LeRoy. I became "Nancy, the Widow." "Nancy, the Widow." Might as well say "Nancy the Leper" or "Nancy the Outcast." Widow. Widow. Widow. I've grown to hate that word!

My heart tells me that there has to be something positive that comes from being a member of this club. Is anything to be gained from sharing my experience with others? I believe there is. I believe there is help, hope and healing for members AND non-members as we journey on this unfamiliar path in our lives.

This book you hold in your hands contains the precious reflections of 7 women who have become members of "the club" known as "Widowhood." None asked to be nominated for this organization but qualified for membership based on only one requirement: the loss of her husband. Each woman deals with grief in her own unique way. Some responses to situations are similar while others are strikingly different. However, three common threads are found throughout each life: these women are all grieving; they are all okay; and, they are all trusting in a Father who has promised each of them that He will never leave or forsake them. That grieving bonds them together as members of a club they did not wish to join. But, at the same time, the faith they hold onto with both hands bonds them to a Father who understands their tears, hears them when they cry out in fear, and loves them through each and every day and every new situation they face without their husbands.

This book is intended for three groups of people: first and foremost, for those women who are widows. Secondly, for those women who will become widows. And thirdly, for anyone who has ever wondered what to say (or not say) to someone who has become a widow.

Perhaps some of these stories that are shared will not touch you at all. Perhaps others will speak directly to your heart. Whatever it may be, it is my prayer that, if you are a member of the club called "Widowhood," you will find hope, encouragement and healing as you experience the deep love of our Father. If you are not yet a member, I pray that this book will, in some way, help you prepare for what may be ahead. And if you know someone who is a widow, it is my prayer that you will glean some insights as to what to say and do, or NOT say and do, for a woman experiencing the "World of the Widow."

Chapter 1

"Nancy"

Jeremiah 29:11 "For I know the plans I have for
you," declares the Lord, "plans to prosper you
and not to harm you, plans to give you hope and a
future." (NIV)

"He's gone, Nanc...He's gone." My brother spoke those words with such precision and...something else...with a moan of hopelessness and helplessness melting into each other. My mind responds "Yes, I see, but please don't stop!" but the words won't come out. I try to say them, but my lips tremble and I feel my chin shaking silently. I can't take my eyes off of the still form on our living room floor. He looks like he's taking a nap! How can that be?! My mind is racing while my thoughts scream to be heard! He can't be dead! But there he is. My brother is a doctor. I am a nurse. We've seen death before. And we both know that we are seeing it now. No more CPR. No more shocking. Stop the IV. Nothing is going to change what we see. My husband of 35 years, the one who made me laugh more than anyone else, the huge hands that reached to hold my slender ones, the smile, the deep voice that I could recognize in a room of 1,000...the love of my life had stepped before our Father with the snap of His fingers.

In an instant I became a part of society known as "The Widowhood." There was no letter in the mail asking me to join, no telemarketer calling with one of those "Have I got a deal for you!" phone calls. Nothing. Just a sudden over-whelming wave of incredible sadness that I would never again, this side of eternity, hear my husband's voice or be squeezed by arms that loved to tickle me, just to hear me yell his name. I did not ask to become a member of the club...but I did not have a choice.

Lesson #1: Eat only if you want to, but never forget to drink water.

The day my husband LeRoy died, people were all over my house...hundreds, I am told. A room full of people no matter where I turned: the living room, kitchen, bedroom. Kind people, loving people, people who were in shock just as I was over my loss. Some were crying. Some were just shaking their heads as if to say "How can this be?" while others thoughtfully carried in armfuls of paper products and food. We as a nation are programmed to celebrate every bit of news that comes our way – good OR bad – with food. Eat because of a birthday, or because of a new job or because of stress or because of NO stress...but eat! I did not want to eat. I only wanted one thing – that my husband could be with me – but that was not going to happen any more. Ever. No more discussion. Final. However, people kept putting food before me. "Eat, Nancy, you need to eat." (No, I don't. I need to throw up. I need to scream. I need my husband. But I do NOT need to eat.) "Here, just a sandwich. I will NOT leave until you eat." I put a grape in my mouth and said "Okay, there you go." I chewed it but it refused to be swallowed. It felt like a brick in my mouth. What to do then? Give it back? The best advice given was from the minister who was going to do the service. He said to no one in particular and yet to everyone: "Nancy doesn't need to eat. She's not going to faint from not having a meal or two. Just make sure she drinks water. Nothing more." His glance at me spoke volumes. His experience as a minister had taught him that not everybody reacts to stress by eating.

Some people react exactly opposite to that. And it's okay. But we lose a tremendous amount of water when we cry and we all must have water to survive. "Jesus answered, "Everyone who drinks this water will be thirsty again, but whoever drinks the water I give him will never thirst." John 4:13, 14 (NIV)

Lesson #2: Realize that our strength comes from our Father and we do not have to be strong in our own power.

The evening my husband passed away, everyone finally left our home about midnight and I fell into bed. I had felt compelled to stay up until the last person left in order to show everyone that I was strong and I would be okay. To say that I was exhausted does not begin to cover how I felt, but the shock of the last several hours glossed over that exhaustion and smothered it in numbness. I laid on my right side, looking over at my husband's pillow, but unable to focus because of the tears. Sleep did not find me during those hours but it was replaced by something else: along with the incredible sadness that I felt was an even more incredible peace that I simply cannot describe. My eyes did not close that night but neither did my Father's. I stayed on His lap all night as He held me in His arms. I could hear His voice over and over: "I am still in control. I have a plan. Trust me, Nancy, trust me." When my sadness gave way to extreme exhaustion and I could hold on no longer, my Father held on to me. And He did not let go.

Lesson #3: When you think you are imparting pearls of wisdom, stop and ask yourself if you would want those "pearls" given to YOU as a present...

The advice that one receives in "the club" of widowhood can be of extreme value or it can just be extreme. Well meaning people want, more than anything, to help. One particular lady approached me about a month after my husband passed away. She leaned over to me, as if sharing wisdom meant only for my ears, and with a pat on my hand, she said "You lost your husband? Get a dog." Now, I am quite certain that my face had a look closely akin to "Are you nuts?" on it, but I simply said "Thank you so much for your advice." She nodded, smiled and walked away, knowing in her heart that she had made my life perfect again. I stared at her back thinking, "Husband and a dog, husband and a dog. How in the world are they similar?" It occurred to me that they both eat on demand and you have to clean up after them on a daily basis. Could that have been what she meant? I haven't asked. And I doubt that I will. Some questions are better left unanswered.

Lesson #4: The only way that you can know how I feel is if you are in my skin, in my mind, in my broken heart. Just say you are sorry. No more. No less.

Another woman came to my home and exclaimed "I know just how you feel." Okay, let me look at you. There you stand with your husband, kids, a great job, no body fat...how can you know how I feel? Give me a hug. Say how sorry you are. Say absolutely nothing. Above all, pray for me. But, unless you are a member in "the club," do not assume you know how I feel. Because you do not.

Lesson #5: It's okay to leave his name in the phone book or on checks or even on return address stickers. It is also okay to change them if you wish. There is an issue of safety and protection if the name remains. But it is not an issue of the law. Do as you so desire.

When you become a member of "the club," you automatically become a name dropper. I'm not talking about someone who is quick to mention the name of someone famous as if they are best friends: "Well, I had lunch at Nick's Place and I sat at a table next to the president of the bank...well, I THINK he was...or at least he had the same hair." Name dropping, to a widow, means that she is immediately encouraged to take her husband's name off any and all documents and papers they possessed together. I went to an appointment with my insurance agent. I had sold a seldom used car and needed to let them know. The agent said "While you are here, do you want to take your husband's name off the insurance?" A very innocent question. A question asked in kindness. I must be ambidextrous because my mind said "NO! I do NOT want his name off the policy. One more way to erase him from my life!" while simultaneously my mouth was saying "Yes, that's a good idea. Thank you." The agent was quick to add "It doesn't have to be done right now. It can wait a while if you wish." I'm sure it was a good idea. Just not to me. Yet another name dropping incident occurred: my husband had been gone 32 weeks and I was on my last pad of checks. As I looked at them..."LeRoy OR Nancy Hughes"...I could not bring myself to order checks without his name. Maybe next time. But not this time.

Lesson #6: **You have my full permission to speak with me, just as you did before I lost my husband. I may be on autopilot inside for a while but my ears still function well on their own.**

It's funny how people react to you when you've lost your husband. It's similar to how people talk to someone who is blind. They lean over to the ear of that person and, with a raised voice, say "HOW...ARE...YOU?" as if the person is also deaf. Not so. That's exactly how a widow is treated. People are well meaning, make no mistake. But rest assured: I am single, NOT senile! I was not diagnosed with Alzheimer's when my husband died. I DID lose a part of myself, but it was not my brain...just my heart...

Lesson #7: **Whether or not to keep your husband's clothes is entirely a personal decision. As long as your closet is not a shrine in his memory that you bow to each day, it's entirely up to you. But only you.**

A well meaning friend called me a few days after my husband's funeral. "I'll be over tomorrow and we'll get rid of LeRoy's clothes," she said. I couldn't help my immediate response: "Why? Why would I do that?" She continued "They will be a constant reminder that he is gone. Every time you look at them you will be reminded of his death. It's much better to get rid of them." My friend has not lost her husband. I tell her as kindly as I can that I have no immediate plans to get rid of his clothes. Maybe later I will do that. Goodwill always needs things. But not right now. She seems to be satisfied with that answer and we hang up. What I don't tell her is that I go into my closet, sit on the floor, and bury my face in his shirts. And cry? Yes, I cry. I grieve. I'm not a masochist, inflicting pain intentionally on myself. I'm pulling his shirts to my face because they smell like him...

and I will keep all his clothes until they no longer carry his scent. Then...maybe then...I will give them away.

Lesson #8: I may appear perfectly healed from my grief and loss on the outside, but don't assume that "what you see is what you get." Sometimes I have a "public" face and sometimes a "private" face. My look depends solely on what I decide to show you and what I think you are able to handle from me.

Several months after my club membership began, I received a call from a caring person concerning a mutual friend who had also lost her husband. "She comes to work crying, she cries off and on during the day, she leaves crying." was the comment. "Can you talk to her? It needs to get better." It struck me as rather odd that I, a recent widow, would be contacted to talk to another recent widow, about getting it all together and moving on with life. I wondered why? Could it be that, because I do not happen to cry in public over my loss, it is assumed that I am now healed of my grief? There is a perception that grief is like a bad cold: 10 days and some TLC and its over. Not so. Not so. I may grieve the rest of my life over the loss of my husband. Oh, life will go on. And I will go on. That's my choice. And that's God's plan. But allow me to show you my hurt and my tears once in a while. And some day, I will allow you to show me yours.

Chapter 2

"Jacque"

Song of Solomon 2:8-17: "Listen! My lover! Look!
Here he comes, leaping across the mountains,
bounding over the hills. My lover is like a gazelle
or a young stag. Look!…See! The winter is past;
the rains are over and gone. Flowers appear on the
earth; the season of singing has come, the cooing of
doves is heard in our land…My lover is mine and I
am his; he browses among the lilies. Until the day
breaks and the shadows flee, turn, my lover, and
be like a gazelle or like a young stag on the rugged
hills." (NIV)

It was one of those marriages that many dream about
but few ever actually find. He is a devoted husband and
father and his family comes before his job or his hobbies
of hunting and fishing. His wife Jacque is petite with dark
hair and a ready smile - a pretty young woman who can't
help but smile and laugh at her husband as he plans joke
after joke just to see that smile. Their son is 2 ½ years old
and they just found out the previous week that this tiny life

Jacque has been carrying for 4 ½ months is a girl – exactly what her husband had prayed for! Life could not be better or more blessed. Then on a fall afternoon as her husband was hunting, Jacque's cell phone rang: "Honey, I've been shot." Her first reaction was the same as almost every other time he has played a joke on her: "Yeah, right." But instantly the line went dead, so she called him back. In a split second, with the force of a searing hot knife being thrust into her heart, Jacque realized that this was no joke but the beginning moments of a horrible nightmare come true. A few hours later she found herself sitting next to her husband's bed in the intensive care unit at the hospital, holding his hand as she whispered her love. From somewhere near her shoulder a doctor quietly told her that there was nothing further they can do to stop her husband's bleeding. A day that began like so many others ended at 9:04 p.m. for Jacque's husband and for her as well. The bleeding in his body could not be stopped. The bleeding in her heart had only begun.

Lesson #1: Please continue to ask me how I am doing. It hurts almost as much if you do not ask. Do not worry about my response. Just ask.

"People stop asking how you are doing," Jacque says. "It's not that they don't want to know. They care very much. They just believe that by asking, they are opening up a painful injury again and again." Friends, acquaintances, family – you remember my husband. You picture the laughing, teasing, always-helping-others, bigger-than-life man. And you saw him with me and our children. You saw the love in his eyes and in his actions and the identical response in mine. So you know I am hurting. But please ask me! Yes, it hurts. Yes, it is unbelievably hard. Yes, I am always looking up, expecting him to walk through the door. Yes, I pray for strength to get though every minute of every day. But something else occurs when you inquire: your kindness helps my heart, ever so slightly, to begin to mend. And to heal. "Therefore, as God's chosen people, holy and dearly loved, clothe yourselves with compassion, kindness, humility, gentleness and patience." Colossians 3:12 (NIV) Shelter me with your clothing.

Lesson #2: Allow me to share this loss with my children in a way I believe they can understand.

Jacque's son was only 2 ½ years old when his father died. He had no concept of death but simply knew that Daddy was not at their home any more. Jacque told him that his daddy was now living with the angels and, if you ask her son, that is exactly what he says. When they go to the cemetery he always yells "Hi Daddy!" as he brings gifts of flowers and a pinwheel to the gravesite. "That way," Jacque says, "he sees the wind blowing the pinwheel and knows that his daddy hears him." You may have ideas concerning how to explain to my children what has happened to their father. They do not need philosophy and long explanations. They simply need to know about God's love and that He will watch over us. Please let me be the one to answer their questions. If I cannot find an answer, I will look to you for advice. "(God is)...A father to the fatherless, a defender of widows." Psalm 68:5 (NIV)

Lesson #3: There will come a time when I begin to smile again. And laugh. And live. Do not mistake these as signs that I am completely healed and through grieving. I am simply trying to allow a little bit of normalcy to slowly find its way back into my life.

Jacque states that one of her husband's best friends said the only way he has made it through this loss was to see her smile once in a while – even though it might be a "fake" smile. It is not required that you laugh or smile in the "Widowhood Club." Indeed, it is an almost impossible feat. Just know that my laughter, if you hear it, is harder on me than on you. I feel guilty. I am in a state of duel membership: One part of me wants to return to a more normal life and yes, to smile. Yet the other part is crying day and night over my loss. As time moves on, other decisions become harder and harder. "Do I go out to eat?" Will someone see me and think that I am "over" my loss? "Didn't she just lose her husband?" they will say. Should I take off my wedding rings? My hand is naked without them. My heart is broken without him. I buy a new dress. But why? My husband will not be there to tell me how great I look...even if I don't. Bear with me as I travel this new path the Lord is designing for me. He knows my name...and my heart. "Even in laughter the heart may ache, and joy may end in grief." Proverbs 14:13 (NIV)

Lesson #4: Encourage me to ask for help. Encourage me to ask for help. Encourage me to ask for help. And, if you are still in doubt, encourage me to ask for help.

There may be a time when the realization that "I cannot do this by myself." hits and you recognize that you need help. There are people everywhere, including friends, family, church family and simple acquaintances who are waiting in the wings to help you. Eaves need to be cleaned out, lawns mowed, oil changed, furniture moved, trees cut down, meetings kept, babysitters called, bills paid, plants watered, boards replaced, rooms painted, food cooked, Christmas lights strung, laundry folded, gardens tilled, prayers lifted. Wonderful people are waiting...thinking... "If only she will ask." So ask.

Lesson #5: Know that I can never repay each of you for all the kindness you have shown me. But I shall spend a good part of my life trying.

Jacque was overwhelmed by the outpouring of love and support when her husband died. She received hundreds of cards and letters. At the funeral, 16 fellow hunters and good friends stood as the eulogy was being read – united in their grief and love for this man. A special auction was held to raise money for the family and a memorial was set up in his name. Meals, baby gifts, cases of diapers, and donations from companies around town as well as from total strangers poured in. As widows, we cannot begin to express our gratitude for what you have done and continue to do for us. We may miss writing a "thank you" card for the food you brought, or the lovely flowers at the funeral or the books of stamps you sent with an encouraging letter. We may forget to tell you how thoughtful your note was to us on a day we really needed it or how much we appreciate the lawn being mowed. But please understand that our children will know about you because we will tell them how you shared your lives with ours. And your love.

"I have not stopped giving thanks for you, remembering you in my prayers." Ephesians 1:16 (NIV)

Chapter 3

"Saundra"

Philippians 4: 6 "Do not be anxious about anything,
but in everything, by prayer and petition, with
thanksgiving, present your requests to God." (NIV)

S aundra had not even the slightest clue of her imminent
initiation into the widow club. She and her husband
had been married 28 years and he was a sports enthusiast
and physically active. They had eaten out with friends one
evening and had had a wonderful time of laughter and conversation. Later in the night, she awoke to her husband saying "I
am really sick. You need to take me to the hospital," which
she did immediately. She found herself sitting, alone, in the
hospital waiting area, thinking "The flu? Something he ate? I
wonder what is wrong?" and praying with all her might. She
had no idea that, a few minutes later, a doctor would come
out and say "I'm sorry. It was his heart. There was nothing
we could do. He's gone." Her immediate club initiation was
followed by "Okay, we need his social security number,
insurance papers, those things." She could only stare. "You
need what? You just told me my husband has died! MY

husband! MY soul mate! MY security! MY life! And you want what?" Thus her journey began into the unchartered territory known as "The Widow."

Lesson #1: Saying "If I can do anything for you, let me know" is always meant in the nicest possible way. But just ask the Lord to SHOW you what you can do for me, and then please do it.

Saundra was in her yard when a man from church came to see her. As he stood in the 8 inch tall grass, he said "If I can do anything at all, just let me know." She thought to herself "I need my lawn mowed. You are standing in the middle of a need that I have. If you cannot see it, maybe it's not something you want to do for me." So she thanked him but said nothing else. And he left thinking that all was well. Perhaps it's a desire to be independent that prevents us from sharing our needs with you. Perhaps it is pride. Maybe it is simply that we do not want to take you away from your family and THEIR needs. Whatever the answer, please know that if you will simply open the eyes of your heart, the Lord will make clear to you what needs a widow has and what you can do to help her. He will also encourage you to pause and wait for her answer…and not leave the tall grass unattended.

Lesson#2: There is no question that you still have your dance partner and I do not. Please refrain from telling me as you spin and twirl around the dance floor why you think .....

"It's better this way."

"I know how you feel."

"At least he didn't suffer."

"Life will go on."

"It will get better with time."

"You'll get married again some day."

"There will be better days ahead."

"You had more years together than most people."
"If you only had MY husband, you wouldn't be so sad."

Perhaps some of those statements are true, perhaps not. Regardless, I only want to know that you are praying for me and I want YOU to know that I will remember to never utter even one of those statements when you lose your dance partner one day. "But I tell you that men will have to give account on the day of judgment for every careless word they have spoken." Matthew 12:36 (NIV)

Lesson #3: Do not sound the alarm if you walk by my home and hear me yelling my husband's name at the top of my lungs. I am not going crazy nor am I hallucinating. I am just venting. Please allow me to be frustrated that there are some things he could fix and some that I could not...and still can't!

The car breaks down. Saundra gets it repaired. It breaks down again. It is repaired again...maybe. The zipper is caught halfway up in the back of her dress and she is late. The electricity is off because of the storm and she cannot find the circuit breaker box. Or a candle. The phone rings for the fourth time and no one is there. The road map makes no sense and she is lost. "Do I mix one part oil with two parts gas or the other way around for my weed eater?" she thinks to herself. She feels really sick. What if it is serious? Does she go to the doctor? What is that sound? Could someone be in her home? I am not helpless. I am just struggling as I try to deal with all the things my husband automatically handled. Do not make light of my club membership. After I learn how to take care of these things (and I WILL learn), you may some day need to call on me for help. And I will be ready.

Lesson #4: While I can talk with you about my loss, I may also need to talk with a counselor and certainly with The Counselor as I heal.

Her daughter delivered her first grandchild almost four years to the day after Saundra joined the club. "My husband was gone; my security was gone," she said. "Faith was replaced with fear. Fear that something might be wrong with the baby or my daughter," she continued. A feeling of panic began to slowly creep through her body until it threatened to suffocate her every waking moment. "Who will be next?" Satan whispered with each passing day. She decided to go to a Christian counselor. What she learned was that she had been so busy consoling others, taking care of all the necessary paperwork surrounding this loss and continuing to work at her job, that she had neglected one very important thing: she hadn't grieved. She also found that she was afraid. Afraid that if she truly "let herself go" and cried over the loss of her husband, she wouldn't be able to stop crying. Her wise counselor suggested she set a time to cry. That may sound preplanned or packaged to you. But in Ecclesiastes 3:4, we are told there is "a time to weep and a time to laugh, a time to mourn and a time to dance." She planned a time to weep. And weep she did. Again and again. But with each time came healing and a comfort and peace from our Wonderful Counselor that one day, there would also be a time to laugh. "Hear my cry, O God, listen to my prayer. From the ends of the earth I call to you. I call as my heart grows faint; lead me to the rock that is higher than I. For you have been my refuge, a strong tower against the foe. I long to dwell in your tent forever and take refuge in the shelter of your wings." Psalm 61:1-4 (NIV)

**Lesson #5: The membership in the "Widowhood Club"
is in the millions. Yet standing shoulder to
shoulder, we are all alone.**

I will continue for a very long time to turn and look for
my husband at my side. But I will be alone. Alone in a crowd,
alone at home, alone at church, alone when I go out to eat.
And even though my head knows I will not see him, my
heart will continue to look for him. I will also continue: to
sleep on his side of the bed. To put his cologne on his pillow.
To keep some of his clothes in the closet. To feel my heart
skip a beat when I see a truck like his. To look up from my
paper and expect him to be smiling at me from his. If I had
chosen this…aloneness…then you would not be obligated to
feel sympathy for me. But this was not of my doing OR my
choice…So continue to pray for me as I struggle through this
desolate, lonely place known as "The Widowhood."

**Lesson #6: Your life will go on as usual after my loss.
Do not assume that mine will do the same.
Because it will not.**

Being driven to the funeral home the day of her husband's
service gave Saundra time to reflect on what had happened
and what lay ahead. But she found herself staring out the car
window. "Look at all these people!" she thought. "They are
going about their business as if everything is okay. Do they
not know that my world is devastated? Don't they know this
is the day of Kenny's funeral?" Once the initial shock of loss
is over, people tend to return to their pre-loss lives. Sympathy
cards that arrived by the hundreds are soon replaced by bills
and credit card promotions. "How are you doing?" phone
calls are replaced with silence. Please do not forget us! As
Christians we know Who holds tomorrow. And, as Paul
Harvey says, "…(we) know the rest of the story." We do not
mourn as the rest of the world, but we ARE mourning. Just

continue, in the weeks and months ahead, to let us know that you care.

"I tell you the truth, you will weep and mourn while the world rejoices. You will grieve, but your grief will turn to joy." John 16:20 (NIV)

Chapter 4

"Betty"

Isaiah 41:13: "For I am the Lord, your God, who takes hold of your right hand and says to you Do not fear; I will help you." (NIV)

Standing in the hospital room, looking at her husband of 63 years as he slept in his clean, antiseptic bed, Betty knew that their marriage here on earth was soon coming to an end. His health had not been as good as they had hoped after his open heart surgery. Now, after 2 ½ months in hospitals, there was no surprise or shock as the end came quietly - only an immense sadness that this man who was bigger than life to so many and loved by even more would no longer be a part of their lives here on earth. It could be argued that there should not be as much grief at this loss as, perhaps, a couple who had only been married a few months or years. However, there is an indescribable loneliness that descends quickly when the person you ate your meals with at 6:00 a.m., noon and 6:00 p.m. every day, the one who shared the same home with you for over 60 years, the one who knew what you were going to say before you said it, the one to whom you could tell absolutely anything and know that he would never repeat it to another…that person is no longer at your side or a part of your life. Betty's membership into the club began in such a fashion.

Lesson#1: If you are my best friend, then you know me better than anyone. Allow me some time and space but do not be afraid to call on me as often as you sense I need that call. Being willing to step into my sadness makes us even closer.

Betty says that one friend in particular, a close friend, has gotten her through the very rough days and months after her husband's death. "I was invited out with a group of friends that my husband and I always went with and I found myself as a single in a room of couples. It was very hard." But, Betty continues, her friend, who knew she was going with the group of couples, sensed her heavy heart and emotional sadness. "I could not have been home more than 10 minutes," Betty said, "when the phone rang. It was Sue." "I just knew tonight had to be very hard for you and that you needed to talk," the voice on the phone said. She understood that her best friend had a need and wanted to be there for her. Proverbs 18:24 (NIV) says "…there is a friend who sticks closer than a brother." Her name is Sue.

Lesson #2: Understand that, at first, all the things I used to do may seem pointless to me. Not forever. But for now.

Activities that Betty says were such a part of her life for years became unimportant when her husband passed away. It was simply because the majority of them involved him. "For a while, all I could think was 'Why entertain?' 'Who cares about the garden?' 'Golfing with friends…no, thank you.'" Betty stated. When the person that we shared our day's activities with for years is no longer with us, we may think "Why bother?" Encourage me to participate in those things that I used to do...golfing, playing bridge, tennis. Just remember that, for me, the rules have changed. And I will have to adapt...without my doubles partner.

Lesson #3: When the last friend has left, the last hug has been offered, the last tear has been shed and I am alone in my home, offer to stay with me. I may need you to stay...I may not. But please make the offer and allow me to make that decision.

Betty says that she was amazed at the outpouring of invitations from family and friends to stay with her after her husband's death. "My grandchildren, even my great grand-children, wanted to stay with me. It gave me such comfort in having them there." Some members of the club feel they can make the move forward to stay by themselves from the beginning. Others want someone there to buffer the silence and loss for a while. I may tell you I am okay by myself and that could very well be true, but just in case I call in the middle of the night, please have your suitcase ready. I am not asking you to take up permanent residence with me but I AM asking you to step into my world – just for a while – as I learn to adjust to a new life and lifestyle without my husband. "But if a widow has children or grandchildren, these should learn first of all to put their religion into practice by caring for their own family and so repaying their parents and grand-parents, for this is pleasing to God." I Timothy 5:4 (NIV)

Lesson #4: The time will come when I am able to focus less on my needs and more on the needs of others. But please understand that right now I need this time of healing to gain strength. Strength from the Lord that I must have in order to some day reach out to the growing number of club members around me.

There will come a point in my grief when I am able to look beyond myself and reach out to others who are hurting from the same emotional pain of loss that I have experienced. And I will begin to see that there are other people like me who are hurting and need understanding, compassion and hope. There is healing in the realization that I can perhaps, in some small way, help to soothe a broken heart or encourage a lonely sister in the club...because I have been there. This process of gaining strength may take weeks or months or even years. But it will happen. Isaiah 40:31 (NIV) states "but those who hope in the Lord will renew their strength. They will soar on wings like eagles, they will run and not grow weary, they will walk and not be faint."

Lesson #5: If you have become a member of this club before me, then more than anyone, you truly know how I am feeling and what I am facing. Please call me. Just knowing that you have entered the pit previously and are slowly but surely climbing out will give me tremendous comfort and encouragement...and hope.

For Betty, having a friend who had "been there" and had already been inducted into the club was a great help to her. "She knew what I was feeling and, at times, exactly what I was thinking because she had taken the steps before me," Betty shares. If you have lost your husband, please send a note or make a phone call to me. So many people say they know how I feel, but they are not members. They do not understand why I cry when I see a certain food in the super-market or hear a song on the radio or smell cologne in the men's section of the department store. They are unable to fathom that these simple things remind me of my husband and the life we shared together...and the loss that separates us now. I need you to reassure me that, while you are also grieving, you have walked this path and you are surviving. And I need to know from you that I, too, will follow in your footsteps and survive. "A cheerful look brings joy to the heart, and good news gives health to the bones." Proverbs 15:30 (NIV)

Chapter 5

"Kay"
❧

Proverbs 31:25: "She is clothed with strength and dignity; she can laugh at the days to come." (NIV)

K ay became a bride at 16 years of age. Her husband was big and strong and could move mountains in her eyes. She went from living at home with her parents to marriage to this man and then children four years later. Her husband owned several horses and was known and highly respected throughout the community and beyond. Side by side they worked raising horses and children, cultivating crops and love. After 31 years of marriage, Kay and her husband were very much in tune with each other's every thought and glance and smile. That is why Kay knew without her husband speaking a word that he was not feeling well and hadn't for some time. She finally convinced him to go to the hospital for a checkup. The news was sudden and suffocating: "You have cancer and you have about 8 weeks to live." But wait! That's not how it's supposed to be! Kay's mind began to spin as she looked at her children and her husband...her life! The doctors were not wrong. Within 8 weeks, Kay was thrown out of her couple's world. Everything comes in two's...but Kay will very quickly face the world – and join the widow-hood club – as one.

Lesson #1: If you do not see tears from me at the funeral, please do not mistake that for an absence of caring. You have no idea what either of us has been through before that event and how many tears we have already shed. Or how many more I will shed in private, alone.

Kay's husband spent the last 8 weeks of his life in a hospital and a wheelchair. She says "At the end, there was a relief in me at knowing that he was no longer suffering. I was unable to cry at the funeral because I knew that, for him, the pain and suffering were over." Watching a loved one dying with an incurable disease is similar to watching the wind blowing the sparks of a fire out of control. You see it happening but you realize as you put out three small embers that three more have sprung up and no matter how hard you try, you are not going to be able to stop the inevi-table destruction. It was not until two weeks after the funeral that the reality of her husband's death hit her. "He's really not coming back!" her mind suddenly screamed. She stated that she began crying and those tears continued for days, weeks, months and years. Although outwardly I may appear calm after my loss, do not assume that the inside follows suit. "...The Lord does not look at the things man looks at. Man looks at the outward appearance, but the Lord looks at the heart." I Samuel 16:7 (NIV)

Lesson #2: What I say might not be as important as what I don't say. Allow the ears of your heart to listen for the unspoken words of mine.

You ask me how I'm doing after the loss of my husband and I say "Fine." While that is what you hear with your physical ears, you know with your spiritual ears that my answer is not completely truthful. Maybe for this moment in this hour of this day, "fine" might cover how I am feeling. But overall, it is merely a prepared answer to a question that is asked of me almost daily. Rather than ask me how I'm doing, let me know that you are praying for me. That you think of me often. That you want to take me out for coffee next Tuesday. Allow me the opportunity to expand on "fine" and to tell you how I am truly feeling. "If a man shuts his ears to the cry of the poor, he too will cry out and not be answered." Proverbs 21:13 (NIV)

Lesson #3: I am a passenger on a boat with no oars. The water is either calm or it is crashing and threatening to submerge everything in its path – including me. I never know when the waves will hit so there is no way for me to prepare you for what you may see. Just be ready to throw me a rope...or at least a paddle.

One day I may seem perfectly "okay" to you. I may be at the supermarket shopping and you notice that I am humming quietly to myself. You think "She's just fine. She is moving on. Things are so much better." You may even mention that in conversation with your friends. The very next day, you may see me in a store and you cannot deny the look of loneliness on my face and the tears threatening to break free. You are perplexed! Is this not the same woman who, only yesterday, was humming? Who seemed to be "getting over" her loss? What in the world is wrong? Nothing. Nothing is wrong at all. On the first day that you saw me, I was in a pool of calm water. I was able to sit on the cushion in the middle of the boat and relax for a few minutes. But the second day? Oh, the second day was one in which the waves struck suddenly without warning and tossed me out of the boat and into the water with such force that I had to fight for air and hold on with the last ounce of strength that I had. When you see me and know that I am struggling to breathe and keep my head above the waves, lift me up to the One who controls water with a word and my life with His love. He is the only life preserver that I need. "...Then he got up and rebuked the winds and the waves, and it was completely calm." Matthew 8:26 (NIV)

Lesson #4: Some day I may choose to date again. That does not mean that my grieving is over. That does not mean that I really didn't love my husband. It DOES mean that I am considering canceling my membership in the club and joining the world of couples once again. Nothing more.

After 12 years of being single, Kay says that she began to pray regularly that the Lord would send her someone that she could share her life with and who shared her beliefs. "I dated very little because it just didn't feel right," she said. But the Lord answered her prayer when she met Bob. "He was exactly the one I had been praying for," she continued. "I fell head over heels in love with him. Bob had lost his wife after 39 years of marriage." If I choose to date again, please do not condemn me for wanting companionship and, yes, love. For wanting someone to sit with me in the evening as we share our day over hot cups of coffee. Someone who likes my broccoli casserole. Someone who can make me laugh again...and who will laugh with me. Someone to hold me and reassure me that we are going to make it. "...if two lie down together, they will keep warm. But how can one keep warm alone?" Ecclesiastes 4:11 (NIV)

Lesson #5: The "firsts" that strike again and again in the widowhood club are extremely difficult. But, as hard as it may be for you to understand, "seconds" can be even tougher to face. Please lift me up for strength and courage to face these steps as I move through my months and perhaps years as a widow.

Entrance into the widowhood club was immediately marked by an instant world of heart wrenching "firsts" for Kay: first Christmas, first birthday, first anniversary, first meal, first winter, first time changing a tire...so many firsts without her husband. But a strange phenomenon occurred: the second year without him was harder than the first. How was that possible? The answer was simple in its complexity. The first year of loss was thankfully covered with a blanket of numbness, indeed, a gift of protection from the Lord. Those raw wounds from her husband's death were bandaged in order to allow her to heal. To try to grasp the full impact of what had occurred caused a tremendous emotional pain. The numbing sensation became a welcome guest because it allowed her to focus on the immediate responsibilities that she faced: children wanting to be fed, bills demanding to be paid, laundry needing to be washed. But as the second year began, the numbness quietly slipped away and was replaced with the reality of membership in the club: her husband was really gone and he was not coming back.

So if my first year of membership has seemed to the onlooker to have passed without incident, remember that I am entering a second year without numbness as my constant companion. Please lift me up as I choose strength and courage to take its place. "I can do everything through Him who gives me strength." Philippians 4:13 (NIV)

Chapter 6

"Linda"

Psalm 23 "The Lord is my shepherd, I shall not want…he restores my soul…Even though I walk through the valley of the shadow of death, I will fear no evil, for you are with me;…" (NIV)

Cancer. Few words can strike more fear into the heart of a human being than that one. Perhaps because one day it is silent and the next, screaming at the top of its lungs. But there it is, in black and white. Tests don't lie. They do not have Linda's name on them, but that of her husband of 48 years. The evidence is presented. And the jury is out only a short time before the verdict is read: "Death," it says. No reduced sentence, no appeal. It is final. And Linda becomes yet another unwilling member in the club she will quickly learn to hate.

Lesson #1: The hardest part of being a widow is…being a widow. There is no easy part.

"I am not lonely…I am empty," says Linda. "There are so many times when I feel like "what's the use?" In my kitchen are large pots and pans. I no longer cook for two. Should I get rid of them? My loaf of bread and carton of milk spoil. Only one uses them now instead of two. I go to the grocery store and find few food items for one. So I buy more bread and milk and bring them home...so they will spoil." I am surviving membership in this club I did not choose to join because I am dwelling in the tent of my God. "For in the day of trouble he will keep me safe in his dwelling; he will hide me in the shelter of his tabernacle and set me high upon a rock." Psalm 27: 5 (NIV)

Lesson #2: Please share your memories of my husband with me. I may cry but there is healing in knowing that you, too, remember him and that he lives on in your heart as well as mine.

Linda's husband was an accomplished carpenter and loved making pieces of furniture for people. She says that friends would see her and comment on a shelf or cabinet that her husband had made them and what good work he did. Still others talked fondly of the hard worker that he was and how he could always be found mowing a lawn or helping someone out without asking for anything in return. Feel free to share your special memories with me. By saying his name out loud, you are helping to keep his memory alive for his children and grandchildren...and for me. "I thank my God every time I remember you." Philippians 1:3 (NIV)

Lesson #3: Remember that when you tell me "We will get together soon," I know the chances are slim to none that you will call. So surprise me!

You feel badly for me. I see it in your eyes as you hug me during the visitation and at the funeral. You want more than anything, at that moment, for me to feel better. So you are quick to offer up a glimmer of hope that some sense of normalcy will again be present in my life. "We will get together soon," you whisper. You are being kind and compassionate and you fully intend to do just that. But days roll into weeks into months. And still no contact. There is a paved road that many travel down. Good intentions are at every crossroad, on every sign. Arriving at the destination is easy. Simply say you will do something and then do not do it! Plan to do it...mean to do it...think about doing it, but do not follow through... Take a deep breath and call me. Allow ME to buy the cup of coffee. I need to talk. And you need to carry out your good intention. "Do not take advantage of a widow or an orphan. If you do and they cry out to me, I will certainly hear their cry." Exodus 22:22-23 (NIV)

Lesson #4: Whether or not you approve of how I am coping with my loss is irrelevant to me. But please do not trivialize my grief. Telling me that "Nobody ever died from grieving" implies that what I am going through is short-lived and therefore unimportant.

Seeing someone grieving tends to make others uncomfortable. And something else occurs: the realization that, sooner or later, we will all meet this same foe...this death. Someday you will be faced with the same decisions that I am facing: when and how to grieve. This grieving process, for me, may continue for weeks, months or even years. The separation from my husband is temporary – of that I am sure. But understand that I may grieve until I see him again...on the other side. "Where, O death, is your victory? Where, O death, is your sting?" I Corinthians 15:55 (NIV)

Chapter 7

"Jo"

Psalm 46:1-2 "God is our refuge and strength, an ever-present help in trouble. Therefore we will not fear, though the earth give way and the mountains fall into the heart of the sea." (NIV)

Jo was thrown into the widow club when she was almost 27 years old and the mother of two little girls. "You need to get to the hospital right away, Jo!" she was told. "An accident, a car accident. It's not good." There she sat in the hospital room with her husband as he took his last breath and she took her first…as a widow. Her mind kept repeating, over and over "This is a dream. It's not really happening." But her eyes were telling her something entirely different. In an instant, her life as she had known it for the last three years was changed forever.

Lesson #1: Allow me to grieve in my own way and time. The stained glass window of my hopes and dreams for the future with my husband has been shattered.

Before Jo and her husband married, they "dated" during the two years he was gone in the service. After he died at the end of October, she fell back into the "he is just away" thinking for a while. That did not last long, because his friends from the service sent Christmas cards and she had to write again and again about the accident and her husband's death. But it did numb the pain of his loss for a little while. Please let us cope with this intense heartache in the way we see fit. It will allow us to gather strength for the days and months ahead of dealing with the reality of going on in life without our husbands.

Lesson #2: Put your words into actions. The old cliché "If you need anything, just give me a call." may make you feel as if you have helped me, but what if I don't have a phone?

When we see someone hurting, many of us feel the need to "make things better" for that person. That's the easy part. The tough part comes when we make the decision to step out of our perfect, orderly, "normal" world and actually DO something for someone no longer in that organized state. Jo says that friends immediately came to her aid. She and her husband had lived in the country on a farm. She knew that she needed to have a farm sale but had no idea where to begin. "Neighbors in our community were amazing," she says. Some friends were auctioneers who took care of the sale. Others helped her move out of her home in the country and into town. Her sister-in-law watched her daughters so she could go to work. Nothing was asked of Jo in return. People simply saw the need and met the challenge. Matthew

25:36 (NIV) says "I needed clothes and you clothed me, I was sick and you looked after me..." Dare we do any less?

Lesson #3: Realize that I am not the only one hurting. Consider my husband's parents, siblings, and friends as well as my children and me. We have all sustained battle wounds from this loss.

It was extremely hard to see the emotional pain that her in-laws were suffering, Jo said. Well meaning people tended to focus on the immediate person who had suffered the loss: the wife. They would go to a sister or brother or parent and ask "How is "she" doing?" without stopping to realize that they are asking that question of someone who is NOT doing any better than "she" is. A father, a brother, a son, an uncle has died...not just a husband. The loss may not seem as important to you, but it is just as painful to them. With his death died, too, their hopes and dreams for that beloved man.

Lesson #4: Allow me to grieve for that which was to be and will never be. For the future that one minute stretched before me with joy and hope and in an instant disappeared forever.

Jo states that the hardest part of being a widow for her was that her little girls did not have a father. He was gone. He would never see them grow up, graduate, get married. No more playing with his children and then, someday, his grandchildren and great grandchildren. Her evenings that had previously consisted of her family laughing and loving together now became a time that she spent rocking her daughters and reading to them. And thanking the Lord that her husband lived on in each of their lives. Know that the laughter will come again. Smiles will return one day to our faces. But there is no timetable or schedule that mandates when that must occur. Watch for it! We may both be surprised. "...weeping may remain for a night, but rejoicing (joy) comes in the morning." Psalm 30: 5 (NIV)

Lesson #5: "Sticks and stones may break my bones but words can never harm me" may be a childish chant but please remember that what you say to me in my loss makes a big difference. My heart is already torn in two. I do not need more pain.

Going back to work helped Jo to focus on those people who came to her for help and not on her situation at home. Or at least she thought that was the case. One woman in particular became angry at Jo when she did not help her as quickly and exactly as she wanted. With a proud toss of her head she informed Jo that she knew why she was a widow: because she was so wicked. Jo drove home and cried. Tears for herself, her small children and her situation. But also, tears for a woman who had intentionally inflicted a wound on her slowly healing heart. "Reckless words pierce like a sword, but the tongue of the wise brings healing." Proverbs 12:18 (NIV)

Lesson #6: If I choose to go to the cemetery often, it's normal. If I choose to go to the cemetery seldom, it's normal. If I choose not to go at all, I am normal.

Jo did not routinely go to the cemetery after her husband died. "I believe that the person is always a part of your life and for me, there was no reason to keep returning to the cemetery," she said. It may be hard for some to go there and it may be equally hard not to go. If you happen to see any of us sitting beside the gravesite and talking about everything going on in our lives, please do not speculate whether or not we are losing our minds. We are not. If you notice that we have chosen not to go regularly to the cemetery, again, no speculation is warranted as to our sanity. In either instance, we have chosen the way that brings a sense of comfort, peace and healing for each of us. And we are okay. "He is not here; he has risen, just as he said." Matthew 28:6 (NIV)

Conclusion

S o there you have it: seven women in a club of millions. Seven women who know what it is like to be thrown in the pit of widowhood and what it is like to survive as they climb out of that pit. The lessons to be learned from each chapter in this book are as varied and unique as the women who present them, yet the similarities remain: all seven women are grieving, all are okay, and all are holding onto the One who will never let go of them.

Whether a woman has been suddenly thrown into the club or has experienced a gradual descent into its membership, the moment of initiation can cause an overwhelming loss of security and saneness because her world has been shaken to its very depths. Everything that she has known up to that moment as safe is rocked with the force of an earthquake and she can not stand against the quake or the aftershocks. The one who protected her and gave her the self-confidence to do anything, the one who was her defense from the world, the one who would have scooped her up and taken her to the place where the quake could not reach…that one – her husband - is gone. And how is each woman handling her membership today in the widow club?

Nancy is completing her first year in the club. She remains at the job she has held for the last 20 years and continues to drive home each day, expecting her husband to be waiting for her. His clothes still hang in their closet, his toothbrush in the bathroom, his smile in her heart. An incredible peace surrounds her as she begins her second year of membership in the club. She believes with all her heart that her Father has a plan for her life and her hope is in Him. Although her legs have been knocked out from under her and her grieving continues... her foundation holds firm in the Lord.

Jacque has moved to a new house and a new job. The home she shared with her husband held too many memories for her and her small son. She is excited to see what the Lord has in mind for her and continually praises Him for her son and new daughter. Jacque has saved some of her husband's belongings for their son when he is older. She intends to make sure that her children know the man who loved them with all his heart. She takes one day, indeed one hour, at a time as her grieving continues and she allows the Lord to direct her life. It's not easy. But she is confident of the One who is in control.

Saundra, who has several years of membership experience in the widow club, still has moments from time to time when unshed tears escape as she considers what a wonderful grandfather her husband would have been. But she has asked the Lord to direct her paths and He has answered her prayer by allowing her the opportunity to go on several missionary trips. She is so thankful to be able to share her faith with people in different countries and to tell them how the Lord has kept His arms around her through the very toughest times.

Betty has resumed some of her activities with friends and family since her club induction over a year ago. She takes every opportunity to share with those around her about a Father's deep love for His children and how He has held on to her and given her peace. She finds a great deal of comfort in sitting in her husband's favorite chair in the evenings and remembering their conversations and laughter. Her grieving continues and there are still tears at her loss but the trust she has in Christ has already prompted her to minister to women who have joined the club after her.

Kay has recently remarried after 13 years of being in the club. She is quick to praise the Lord for the happiness she is now experiencing. "When you put your life in His hands," Kay says, "and trust Him with everything, the Lord does tremendous things. He answers your prayers above and beyond anything you can imagine."

Linda is entering her second year in the widowhood club. She states "I have good days and bad days and sometimes a combination of both." Her loss at times seems to be almost overwhelming but her Father wraps His arms of love around her as she lives and learns a new role without the presence of her best friend. "I cannot imagine how I could keep going without the Lord to lean on," she says. And she continues to hold fast to the One who will not let go.

Jo has been remarried for 44 years after her initiation into the club. Her husband has been a wonderful father and friend to her daughters and to their grandchildren and great grandchildren. Her trust in a Father who will never let her down is apparent to all who know her. She lives her faith every moment of every day.

And where was our Father when these ladies were being thrown into the pit of the widow club? Where was He when they were crying out for rescue from this membership? He was crying with them. He was holding out His arms to them. He was whispering their names. He was reassuring them "Never will I leave you; never will I forsake you." Hebrews 13:5 (NIV) And He was quietly reminding them that He DOES have a plan and that He is STILL in control.

I do not like my life as a widow right now. But therein lays the key: I don't HAVE to like it. What I need to do… what I MUST do…is trust the One who made me. Trust the

One who died for me. Trust the One who whispers MY name in the middle of this horrible storm that batters me around and threatens to leave my heart bruised and bleeding. And I need to praise Him - for His love, for His mercy, and for His peace in the middle of this trial.

And where is God when your storm hits? When the winds knock you to your knees and the suffocating force of the situation threatens to drown you in the pit of widowhood? He is there…in the middle of the storm…by your side. He is the Voice that whispers "Hold onto me! We will get through this!" He is the Thunder that shouts "Give me your hand and I will PULL you through!" He is the Father who weeps as you weep, who holds you in His arms. He is the One who wipes the tears from your eyes and repeats, over and over, "I have a plan. Trust me with everything you have and I will give you everything you need." And how could He possibly know how we feel? Because He has been there. Because He watched His Son take His last breath, watched His eyes close in death. Because just as He raised His son Jesus from the grave, He will do no less for His children.

May we encourage all of you to stand firm and hold tight to our Father! The grieving may continue for months or years but the words of our Father will continue for eternity. Do you feel like your strength is almost gone? Psalm 73:23-24 (NIV) says "Yet I am always with you; you hold me by my right hand. You guide me with your counsel…" Are there moments when it seems that no one wants to listen to your sadness? Psalm 62:8 (NIV): "Trust in him at all times, O people; pour out your hearts to him, for God is our refuge." Do you need a place to hide when the pain of your loss threatens to overwhelm you? Consider Psalm 91:1-2 (NIV): "He who dwells in the shelter of the Most High will rest in the shadow of the Almighty. I will say of the Lord, "He is my refuge and my fortress, my God, in whom I trust." Does it seem like no one hears your cry for help? Read Psalm 40:

1-2 (NIV): "I waited patiently for the Lord; he turned to me and heard my cry. He lifted me out of the slimy pit, out of the mud and mire; he set my feet on a rock and gave me a firm place to stand."

We are survivors in a club not of our choosing. It is our prayer that those of you who have joined the ranks of widowhood or who will someday become members as we are will never lose sight of the One who will guide you through. May you find comfort and compassion in His words of encouragement and love as you travel this path of "The Widow":

"But those who hope in the Lord will renew their strength. They will soar on wings like eagles; they will run and not grow weary, they will walk and not be faint." Isaiah 40:31(NIV).

Printed in the United States
105194LV00001B/289/A